A Cas[...]
Design[...]

"You're not going to believe this!" Deirdre said. "You're just not going to believe it!"

"Believe *what*, Deirdre?" Nancy asked.

"I went to Mrs. Corwin's classroom this morning to ask her a question," Deirdre said, "and that's when I saw her crying."

"Juliana can't find our designs!" Nadine said. "They've disappeared!"

"That shouldn't be a problem. Mrs. Corwin scanned the designs and e-mailed them to Juliana," Nancy said. "The file will still be on her computer."

Deirdre shook her head. "Mrs. Corwin and Juliana were going to retrieve the file, Nancy, but a virus must have corrupted it." She let out a moan. "My life is over."

Join the CLUE CREW
& solve these other cases!

NANCY DREW

#29 AND THE CLUE CREW

Designed for Disaster

By Carolyn Keene

Illustrated by Macky Pamintuan

Aladdin
New York London Toronto Sydney

🪔 ALADDIN

An imprint of Simon & Schuster Children's Publishing Division

1230 Avenue of the Americas, New York, NY 10020

First Aladdin paperback edition May 2011

Text copyright © 2011 by Simon & Schuster, Inc.

Illustrations copyright © 2011 by Macky Pamintuan

All rights reserved, including the right of reproduction in whole or in part in any form.

ALADDIN PAPERBACKS and related logo, NANCY DREW, and NANCY DREW AND THE CLUE CREW are registered trademarks of Simon & Schuster, Inc.

For information about special discounts for bulk purchases, please contact Simon & Schuster Special Sales at 1-866-506-1949 or business@simonandschuster.com.

The Simon & Schuster Speakers Bureau can bring authors to your live event. For more information or to book an event contact the Simon & Schuster Speakers Bureau at 1-866-248-3049 or visit our website at www.simonspeakers.com.

Designed by Lisa Vega

The text of this book was set in ITC Stone Informal.

Manufactured in the United States of America 0411 OFF

2 4 6 8 10 9 7 5 3 1

Library of Congress Control Number 2010928808

ISBN 978-1-4169-9439-8

ISBN 978-1-4424-2380-0 (eBook)

CONTENTS

CHAPTER ONE

Mystery Girls!

On Monday morning Mrs. Corwin, a River Heights Elementary School art teacher, said, "I'm putting you in teams of three. You're going to draw pictures of anything you think would be really cool for you and your friends to wear."

The girls cheered. The boys all just looked at one another.

"I think you'll be very excited about what I'm planning to do with your designs too," Mrs. Corwin added, "but I need them all by Friday."

Nancy Drew turned to her two best friends, who were also her art-table partners, cousins Bess Marvin and George Fayne, and said,

"That's what's so great about our school. We get to do things like this."

Bess nodded. "I know," she said. "We have a cousin in Texas, and all he does in his art class is draw pictures of cactus plants."

Nancy laughed. "Really?" she said.

George giggled. "Not really. But his art class is definitely not as cool as ours."

"Why do we boys have to do this?" Quincy Taylor asked Mrs. Corwin. "It's a *girl* thing!"

"No, it's not," Deirdre Shannon said. "One of my favorite designers is a man. I try to wear his clothes all the time. A lot of men are famous fashion designers, Quincy."

"And remember I said you can design *anything* you want to," Mrs. Corwin reminded them. "That means sportswear like tracksuits, basketball uniforms, and swim trunks. *Anything!*"

"Yeah, but what if some of the other guys in school find out about this and start making fun of us?" Peter Patino said. "What are we going to do *then*?"

"Oh, you guys, I can't believe it," Mrs. Corwin said. She let out a big sigh. "I'll tell you what. Instead of putting your *real* names on your designs, you may use a designer label. It should be something snappy that'll catch a buyer's attention, and it will be something only the team members and I will know. How's that?"

The boys all looked at one another and shrugged. "Okay, we'll do it," they grumbled in unison.

"May we use both our names *and* a designer label?" Nancy asked. "We want a snappy label, but we also want people to know who we really are."

"Oh, Nancy, that's a super idea," several of the girls said.

"Of course!" Mrs. Corwin told them.

With the teams chosen, everyone talked for the next several minutes about their designer-label names.

"I think ours should be Mystery Girls!" Bess suggested. "I can see that on jeans and tops and—"

"I absolutely adore that," Deirdre said from the next table. She thought for a minute. "I think we'll be Lucky Girls!"

Nancy, George, and Bess rolled their eyes. Deirdre could be such a copycat sometimes, but that was okay since their designs would be different.

"Do you think we'll make any money from this?" George asked.

"Money!" Katherine Madison said. "You mean, like, *real* money?"

"Are you kidding me?" Nadine Nardo exclaimed. "Fashion designers are all rich." She took a deep breath and exhaled. "I could be a millionaire before I'm in the fifth grade!"

Quincy looked up. "Well, then I'm interested too because I'm not looking forward to all the chores Mom said she has planned for me during the summer if I want an allowance."

The class laughed, but Nancy noticed that all the boys' teams had now huddled together to talk about what they were going to do.

When the recess bell rang twenty minutes later, Bess leaned over to Nancy and George and said, "I wonder what Mrs. Corwin is planning to do with our designs."

"That's funny," Nancy whispered back. "I was just thinking the same thing."

As they headed out of the art classroom, Deirdre and Katherine came up behind them.

"I wonder what Mrs. Corwin will do with our designs," Deirdre whispered.

George grinned knowingly at Nancy and Bess.

"We have to find out," Katherine said. "It could affect our new careers!"

Nancy thought about it for a minute. *Should the Clue Crew try to solve the mystery right away,* she wondered, *or should we just wait until Mrs. Corwin tell us?*

ChaPTER TWO

Rhes!

On Friday morning all the fashion designs were turned in by the girls *and* the boys, and now everyone was waiting to hear what Mrs. Corwin was going to do with them.

Nancy, Bess, and George had decided not to spoil Mrs. Corwin's surprise by trying to solve the mystery.

"I have a dear friend from college who's a fashion designer in New York City," Mrs. Corwin told them. "She wants to start a new clothing line, so she's agreed to look at your designs to see if they'd fit with what she has in mind. I'm going to scan them and then e-mail them to her this morning."

"Oh, wow!" Nancy said. She looked at Bess and George, whose eyes were wide with surprise. "Can you believe it?"

"Never in a million years!" Bess said.

"When will we know?" Deirdre asked.

"Monday morning," Mrs. Corwin said.

During the weekend all anyone could talk about were the fashion designs.

When Monday morning finally arrived, Nancy, Bess, and George hurried into Mrs. Corwin's room and took their seats.

"Class, this is my wonderful friend, Juliana Marigold," Mrs. Corwin announced, "and the young lady next to her is Nicole Whitcomb, a fashion model. She's in the third grade too!"

Bess looked at Nancy. "I didn't know girls our age could be fashion models," she whispered.

Juliana smiled at the class. "I absolutely adore all your designs," she said.

The girls cheered.

Mrs. Corwin held up her hand for silence.

"Unfortunately, I can only use about half of them," Juliana added.

There were several groans.

Some of the boys said, "I hope you don't use ours!"

"I'm sorry that I had to make a choice," Juliana said. She consulted a piece of paper she was holding. "I'm using the designs from Nancy's team, Deirdre's team, and Quincy's team."

"Let's give those teams a hand," Mrs. Corwin said.

Everyone applauded politely.

"Each item of clothing will have 'Rhes!' embroidered on it with the subdesign label below." Juliana walked to the chalkboard and wrote *Rhes!* Beneath that, she wrote *Mystery Girls!*

Nancy, Bess, and George gasped.

"This is a dream come true," Bess breathed.

"Excuse me, what does 'Rhes!' mean, Juliana?" George asked.

"River Heights Elementary School!" Juliana said.

"Cool!" the class said.

Bess turned to Nancy. "Everyone in the world will know about our school," she said.

"We're going to be rich!" Nadine said.

"I think my ONITAP designs are cooler than the ones you chose, Juliana," Amanda Johnson said. "I feel cheated."

Everyone turned to stare at Amanda.

"I could have been rich too!" Amanda added. "It's not fair."

"Amanda, please," Mrs. Corwin said. "We're going to discuss that in just a minute."

Nancy turned to Bess and George. "What's wrong with Amanda?" she whispered. "She's never acted like that before."

Bess and George shrugged.

"None of you will be getting rich," Mrs. Corwin said. "Instead, Juliana is going to make a big donation to our school for the use of the designs. No one in the class will receive any money."

Everyone looked at one another. Was that fair?

Mrs. Corwin looked at Juliana. "I think you can explain this better than I can," she said.

"I know you may be disappointed, but it would be difficult for any of you to enter into a legal agreement because you're not old enough," Juliana said, "and second of all, it would be very difficult for you to sell only a couple designs to any fashion house. At least this way you will have a connection to the industry that you can use when you get older."

Nancy noticed that a few people still seemed unhappy.

"Juliana and I also have another surprise that we'll tell you in the morning," Mrs. Corwin said. "You'll never guess what it is, either!"

ChAPTER ThREE

The Missing Designs

"The fashion world is coming to River Heights!" Juliana announced the next morning. "That's my new surprise. I'm going to debut my 'Rhes!' clothing line in your school auditorium!"

There was a collective gasp from the class. Nancy could tell that even the boys were surprised.

Deirdre's hand shot up. "Juliana! Juliana! Juliana!"

"Yes?" Juliana said.

"Does that mean that River Heights will be just like New York, Paris, and Rome during their fashion weeks?" Deirdre asked breathlessly.

Juliana nodded. "As close as we can make it,"

she said. "There will be national and international coverage of the event by fashion magazines and television crews!"

"Models walking the runway and all that?" Bess said.

Juliana nodded again. "And speaking of *that*, let me introduce the rest of my models, who just arrived this morning," she said.

Just then a side door opened and three girls and one boy walked inside. They all wore sunglasses.

"You've already met Nicole, who accompanied me, and now I want you to meet Felicity, Elizabeth, Marissa, and Cory," Juliana said.

With that, Elizabeth, Marissa, and Cory paraded in front of the class the way they would walk on the runway during the fashion show, swinging their hands back and forth.

"What's wrong, Felicity?"

Juliana asked. "Why are you just standing there?"

Felicity rolled her eyes. "I don't feel well," she said.

Juliana sighed but didn't say anything.

After the other three models had paraded back and forth several times, they left the room. Felicity hurried to catch up.

"I'll see you in the auditorium in a few minutes!" Juliana called after them.

Bess looked at Nancy and George. "You can

actually feel the electricity in the air," she said.

"Yeah, and if you touched Felicity, you'd probably get shocked," George said. "She definitely doesn't want to be here."

Juliana turned back to face the class. "As promised, there's still one more surprise," she said. "I'm planning to have some of *you* model your designs for the show."

There was a loud shriek from some of the girls.

"Modeling is a perfect job for good-looking guys like me," Quincy said.

"Don't flatter yourself, Quincy," Nadine said. "My mother told me that modeling agencies hire all kinds of models, not just people who look like movie stars."

"Quincy doesn't look like a movie star, Nadine," Peter said. He grinned. "You need glasses."

"That's not what I meant, Peter!" Nadine said. "Modeling agencies hire *real* people too."

"Well, class, I think we're getting off the subject," Mrs. Corwin said. "What we need to do now is start planning for the big event. It'll take all of us working together to pull it off."

"You can do it," Juliana assured them. "I need to go to the auditorium now, but Nicole has agreed to stay with you to answer any questions you might have." She smiled at Nicole. "Nicole is a natural. She doesn't need as much practice as the others."

Nicole smiled back. "Thank you, Juliana," she said.

When the bell rang to signal the end of art class, Deirdre balanced her art book on top of her head and started walking out of the room.

"What in the world are you doing?" George asked.

"I'm doing what models all over the world do, George," Deirdre said. "I'm practicing my runway walk."

"With a book on your head?" George said.

"I suggested it to her," Nicole said. "I just want to make sure you know all our secrets."

"Well, that is nice of you, Nicole," Nancy said.

"I didn't want to say anything, but unlike you . . ." Bess paused. In a whisper she continued, "Those other models seem kind of stuck-up."

Nicole made a face. "Yeah, they can be," she agreed. "But never mind. In modeling school we always practiced our runway walks with a book on top of our head to get proper balance and good posture." Addressing everyone who was around her, she added, "I'd advise you to do the same. Remember that there will be people from all over the world here photographing you."

For the rest of the day, under Nicole's direction, everyone on the three winning design teams walked around balancing books on their heads. From time to time some of the fourth and fifth graders thought it was funny to try to knock them off, but after a while they just gave up. In fact, by the time school was out, Nancy had noticed that a lot of the kids in the other classes were doing the same thing.

When Nancy mentioned that to Bess and George on the way home, George said, "Oh yeah! Modeling fever hit our school big-time. I overheard several fifth graders talking about how much better they would have been doing it than us."

"Oh yeah, right!" Bess said.

The next morning, just as Nancy and the Clue Crew entered Mrs. Ramirez's classroom, Deirdre, Nadine, and Katherine ran up to them. They had stricken looks on their faces.

"Uh-oh, something's wrong," Nancy whispered.

"You're not going to believe this!" Deirdre said. "You're just not going to believe it!"

"Believe *what*, Deirdre?" Nancy asked.

"I went to Mrs. Corwin's classroom this morning to ask her a question," Deirdre said, "and that's when I saw her crying."

"Juliana can't find our designs!" Nadine said. "They've disappeared!"

Deirdre whirled around. "Excuse me! This is my story!" she said. "I'm the one who heard it first!"

"I'm sorry," Nadine said. "It's just that I'm so upset!"

"*You're* upset?" Deirdre said. "It's my life we're talking about here!"

"What happened exactly?" Nancy asked.

Deirdre let out an exasperated sigh. "All of our incredibly wonderful fashion designs have disappeared," she said. "And Juliana's seamstresses need the designs to start sewing the clothes."

"That shouldn't be a problem. Mrs. Corwin scanned the designs and e-mailed them to Juliana," Nancy said. "The file will still be on her computer."

Deirdre shook her head. "Mrs. Corwin and Juliana were going to retrieve the file, Nancy, but a virus must have corrupted it." She let out a moan. "My life is over."

"You'll recover, Deirdre," Nancy said. She

turned to Bess and George. "Still, there's something really suspicious about this. We need to get to the bottom of it right away."

"Well, I'm calling an emergency meeting of the River Heights Fashion Models Club for that very reason," Deirdre announced.

The Clue Crew looked at her.

"What's that?" Nancy asked.

"We've never heard of it," Bess and George said in unison.

"We models need a club where we can discuss our careers and solve any problems that arise, such as what happened to our designs, so I'm starting one right now," Deirdre said.

Nancy rolled her eyes.

"You all need to be at my house tonight at seven o'clock!" Deirdre added.

Since no one in Mrs. Ramirez's class could think of anything else except the disappearance of the fashion designs, she decided to show a DVD about volcanoes.

Halfway through it, though, Nancy noticed Nadine's mother at the door, motioning to Mrs. Ramirez. For a few minutes Mrs. Nardo whispered something in Mrs. Ramirez's ear, but then Mrs. Nardo started waving her hands around and shaking her head. Nancy purposely knocked a pencil onto the floor so she'd have to get out of her seat to pick it up. The pencil landed close to the door, but not close enough for Nancy to hear more than the words "Nadine" and "wonderful model." Just as Nancy got back to her seat, Mrs. Ramirez returned to the front of the room.

Nancy could tell she was upset about something. *I wonder what's going on?* she thought.

That evening only the girl models showed up at the emergency meeting of the River Heights Fashion Models Club.

Deirdre opened with, "As president, I think we should hire Nancy Drew and the Clue Crew to look into this crime."

Nancy gave Bess and George a puzzled look. "We don't know that it's actually a *crime* yet, Deirdre," she said.

"Oh, it's a crime, all right," Deirdre assured everyone. "This whole thing smells fishy to me."

"We agree!" the other members said.

"You will certainly be paid for your work," Deirdre said, looking directly at Nancy, Bess, and George. "Just send the bill to our treasurer."

"What am I going to do with it?" Katherine asked. Nancy thought she looked really nervous. "I only get a small allowance."

"You don't have to pay for it personally, Katherine," Deirdre explained. "We'll use our club dues."

"We don't pay dues," Nancy said.

"Well, we should!" Deirdre said.

Nancy rolled her eyes at Bess and George. "We don't charge for our investigations, Deirdre," she said, "so why don't we just move on?"

"Well, all right, but I want you to be serious about this," Deirdre said.

"We're always serious about solving crimes, Deirdre," Bess said.

"Yeah, Deirdre," George said. "You don't have to worry about that."

"What if Juliana isn't telling the truth?" Katherine said. "What if she just wants to claim the designs as her own?"

"I can believe she'd do that!" Nadine said. "I don't think she really likes us—especially me!"

Suddenly Nancy remembered what she had overheard Mrs. Nardo say. *Did Juliana make negative comments about Nadine?* she wondered. *Was Juliana really not as nice as everyone thought she was?*

"I think that makes Juliana our number one suspect, Nancy," Deirdre said.

Nancy nodded. "We'll talk to her tomorrow morning," she said.

Chapter Four

Too Many Coincidences

On Friday morning when Nancy, Bess, and George walked into Mrs. Corwin's classroom, Mrs. Corwin and Juliana were standing at the front, a big smile on each of their faces.

"How can they be so happy?" Bess whispered.

"That's what I was wondering too," Nancy whispered back. "There's nothing funny about the missing fashion designs."

"Well, if you ask me . . . ," George started to say, but Mrs. Corwin said, "Class, Nicole found the missing designs! All is well!"

There was an audible gasp from the class.

Nancy looked at Bess and George. "I guess Juliana is no longer a suspect!" she said.

Bess and George nodded.

"My modeling career has been saved!" Deirdre announced.

"Where were they?" Nancy asked.

"That's the strangest thing," Juliana said. "They had fallen behind a filing cabinet in one of the dressing rooms." She shook her head. "I'm just positive I looked there, but I must not have looked carefully. I'm certainly glad Nicole dropped her pen and that it rolled behind that particular filing cabinet, or we'd still be searching for them."

Nadine raised her hand. "We thought someone stole them!" she said. She turned to Nancy, Bess, and George. "Our River Heights Fashion Models Club even hired the Clue Crew to investigate."

Juliana looked at her. "Oh my goodness, I can't imagine why anyone would do something like that."

Nancy opened her mouth to speak, but Deirdre said, "Well, those designs are worth a fortune, Juliana. We were desperate. We just couldn't sit by and do nothing."

Mrs. Corwin held up her hand. "Well, Juliana does have something to say that may disappoint several of you," she said.

"Oh no!" Bess whispered. "Something new every day!"

"I have an agreement with a professional modeling agency in New York City," Juliana said, "and Felicity reminded me this morning that I can't have more River Heights models than professional models in the show." She let out a big sigh. "So I can only use *five* of you."

Bess looked at George and Nancy. "That Felicity is a real troublemaker," she whispered.

Nancy and George nodded.

"Who will they be?" Deirdre said. "Who will they be?"

George raised her hand. "I'll be happy to—"

Bess grabbed George's hand and pulled it down. "My cousin thought you were talking about running in the New York City Marathon, Juliana," she said. "She forgot you were talking about the River Heights Fashion Show and how incredibly important it is to some of us!"

Juliana and Mrs. Corwin gave Bess funny looks.

"Well, we're going to decide that by secret ballot, Deirdre," Mrs. Corwin said.

That seemed to satisfy everyone.

After Juliana left to go back to the auditorium, Mrs. Corwin passed out blank pieces of paper. "Write out five names," she told the class. "One of the models has to be a boy."

Fifteen minutes later the ballots had been turned in and counted.

"Here are the results," Mrs. Corwin said. "Nancy, Bess, George, Deirdre, and Quincy!" She looked up at the class. "Is everyone satisfied?"

"Yes," the class answered. George groaned.

Nancy looked at Nadine. She didn't seem disappointed.

"No!" Amanda Johnson shouted.

Everyone turned to look at her. Amanda had never before been so negative about everything.

"I am still very upset that my ONITAP designs weren't chosen," Amanda said. "I think they're better than everyone else's."

"I'm sorry, Amanda," Mrs. Corwin said. "Juliana's decision was based solely on what she thought would sell the best."

Nancy looked at Bess and George. "Her designs weren't bad," she said, "but where in the world did she get 'ONITAP' as a designer label?"

"I still think it's all really unfair," Amanda said.

At that moment the classroom door opened, and Nicole said, "We're ready for the River Heights models!"

With Nicole in the lead, Nancy, Bess, George, Deirdre, and Quincy headed to the school auditorium.

When they got there, all the other models—except Felicity—gave the River Heights models brilliant smiles.

Felicity said, "I hate this town!"

Juliana gasped. "Felicity! That's a terrible thing to say!"

Deirdre turned around and whispered to Nancy, Bess, and George, "Those smiles they gave us are so fake! I'll show them a *real* modeling smile."

"I know," Bess agreed. "Nicole is the only nice one of the group."

For the next several minutes Juliana explained how the fashion show would work, and then she said, "We start rehearsals first thing on Saturday morning. You all need to be here!"

On Saturday morning Nancy, Bess, and George got permission to ride their bikes to River Heights Elementary School.

"I can't believe it's finally here," Nancy said

as they headed toward the auditorium. "This is incredible!"

"Maybe not," George said. "Look."

Nancy and Bess turned to where George was pointing. Mrs. Corwin was standing at the door to the auditorium. Juliana was sobbing on her shoulder.

"Oh no," Nancy said. "This doesn't look good."

When the three girls reached Mrs. Corwin, Nancy said, "What's the matter?"

Mrs. Corwin told them. Some of the clothes for the fashion show were missing—all of them were designs by the River Heights models!

"We can't cancel," Juliana sobbed. "It'll ruin my name."

"We won't cancel," Nancy assured her. She looked at Mrs. Corwin. "You have copies of our designs, so I'll show them to our housekeeper, Hannah. She sews really well, and my dad can help her."

"Our parents will take care of our designs too," Bess said. She turned to George. "Right?"

"Right! And the same goes for Deirdre and Quincy, I'm sure!" George said. "With our parents helping, we'll get it done!"

"Oh, thank you, thank you, thank you," Juliana said. She turned to Mrs. Corwin. "Well, let's start the rehearsal. We'll do what we can."

As Mrs. Corwin and Juliana headed into the auditorium, Bess held back. "These can't just be coincidences," she whispered.

"I agree," Nancy said. She thought for a minute. "And the thief has to be someone here at school," she added. "So when we're finished, let's do a quick search of the auditorium."

"Good idea," George said. "We need to solve this mystery before anything else awful happens!"

ChaPTER FiVE

The Top Suspects

After dinner that night the Clue Crew met at Nancy's house. The search of the auditorium had produced nothing.

"Let's write out the names of our top suspects," Nancy said. "Who are the people we think most want the fashion show to fail?"

"Do you still think we should dismiss Juliana as a suspect?" Bess asked. "Maybe she didn't expect anyone to find our designs behind that filing cabinet, so now she's hidden some of the clothing instead."

Nancy thought for a minute. "Well, my instinct tells me she's not guilty," she said, "but I suppose that until we actually solve the mystery, we should at least call her 'a person of interest.'"

"Oh yeah, that's good, Nancy," George said. "You hear it all the time on television."

Nancy, Bess, and George each started to write their list of names in their case notebooks.

When they finished, Bess read her list. "Amanda and Felicity."

"Me too!" George said. "I didn't have them in that order, but they both made my list."

"But I have a third name," Nancy said.

Bess and George looked at her. "Who?" they asked.

"Mrs. Nardo," Nancy told them.

"Nadine's mother?" George said.

Nancy nodded. She told them what she heard when Mrs. Nardo was talking to Mrs. Ramirez during the volcano movie.

"That's weird," Bess said.

"That's what I thought too," Nancy told them. "And then right after that, Nadine wasn't picked to be a model."

"But the models were chosen by a class vote,"

George said. "Juliana didn't have any say in the selection."

"That might not make any difference to Mrs. Nardo," Bess said. "Criminals always believe what they want to believe."

"Well, should we start by questioning Mrs. Nardo?" George asked.

Nancy shook her head. "As much as I hate to say it, I think we should start with Amanda," she said. "She's shown us a side of her we've never seen before."

Bess and George nodded.

"Amanda has really been pushy about her ONITAP designs," Bess said. "Maybe she decided that if her designs weren't going to be part of the fashion show, then *nobody's* designs were!"

"It certainly looks that way," Nancy said.

George shook her head in disbelief. "Who would ever have thought that Amanda Johnson was a criminal?" she said.

"Well, we don't know that for sure, George," Nancy said. "I'll admit that the evidence certainly points in her direction, but we need to keep an open mind."

"Nancy's right," Bess said.

"Sorry," George said. She sighed. "It's just that the fashion show is so important to our school that I can't believe any of our classmates would try to destroy it."

Since it was still light out, the girls got permission to go to Amanda's house on their bicycles. When they got there, Amanda and her mother were just getting out of their car.

"Hey, Nancy, Bess, George!" Amanda shouted. "What brings you here?"

"That's the friendliest she's sounded in a couple weeks," Bess whispered.

"We just wanted to talk to you about something, if you have the time," Nancy said.

Amanda turned to her mother. "Do you need help with the bags?" she asked.

"No, sweetheart, that's fine," Mrs. Johnson said. "Ask your father to come out. You run along and visit with your friends."

Nancy, Bess, and George followed Amanda inside. Amanda gave her father a hug, told him that her mom wanted his help bringing in the groceries, and then led the way to her room.

"Sit anywhere that's comfortable," Amanda said as she fell onto her bed. "What's up?"

Nancy sat down in a purple canvas sling chair. "You've been acting kind of weird in art class lately," she said. "What's up with you?"

Amanda blushed. "Well, it's just that, uh, well . . ."

"We're sorry your ONITAP designs weren't chosen," Bess said.

"But where did that name come from?" George asked. "It's kind of strange."

"Well, it, uh, just sort of came to me,"

Amanda said, "you know, like a vision, something like that."

"Amanda, are you trying to destroy the fashion show?" Bess asked.

"No! Of course not!" Amanda said. She let out a long sigh. "I was just doing Peter a favor."

"Peter?" Nancy said. "Peter Patino?"

Amanda nodded. "I'm surprised nobody figured it out," she said. "'ONITAP' is 'Patino' spelled backward."

Nancy looked embarrassed. "You're right," she said. "We should have figured that out."

"I don't understand," George said.

"Peter has always wanted to be a fashion designer," Amanda explained, "but he was too embarrassed to let people know."

"That's silly," Bess said.

"It sure is," George agreed.

"Do you think Peter is trying to destroy the fashion show?" Nancy asked.

"No way," Amanda said. "He plans to show his designs to all the people who'll be there."

"Well, we can cross you off our suspect list," Nancy said.

"We didn't want you to be guilty, Amanda," George said, "but we had to ask."

"Don't worry," Amanda said. "You didn't hurt my feelings."

Nancy, Bess, and George stood up.

"Maybe you should call Peter and tell him we know," Bess suggested. "Tell him we also hope a lot of people like his designs."

"I'll do that," Amanda said. "Anyway, he was already feeling kind of guilty for asking me to do what I did."

Outside, Nancy said, "We have two more suspects to talk to, and we don't have that much time left before the world comes to River Heights for the fashion show!"

ChaPTER Six

Excuses and Alibis

The next morning Mrs. Ramirez said, "Nancy, Bess, George, Deirdre, and Quincy, Mrs. Corwin needs you in the auditorium to rehearse for the fashion show. I'll let you take your spelling quiz after school."

Bess turned to Nancy. "I had forgotten about that quiz," she whispered.

"Me too," Nancy said. "This will give us a chance to look over the words before we take it."

As the five of them headed toward the audi-torium, Deirdre said, "I'm glad our parents could make the missing clothes last night."

George nodded. "Mom delivered all of our set

this morning," she said. "She and Dad didn't get much sleep."

"Hannah was still in bed when I left this morning. I felt really sorry for Dad, though," Nancy said. "He had to be in court early for a trial."

"Who's causing all these problems?" Quincy asked.

"That's what we're still trying to find out," Nancy said.

"But it's not Amanda!" Bess chimed in.

"We know. She's telling everyone in school that she finally confessed to the Clue Crew," Deirdre said. She shook her head. "I'm surprised you three didn't figure it out the first day. 'ONITAP,' 'Patino'! Really!"

"I don't know why Peter should be embarrassed about *designing* clothes," Quincy said. "Look at me. I'm *modeling* them."

When they reached the auditorium, they headed toward where Mrs. Corwin was standing with Juliana and the New York models.

"Oh, kids! Thank you so much!" Juliana said. "I don't know how the show could have gone on without all your help."

"You're welcome," Nancy said. "Our parents were all glad to do what they could."

"Some of our neighbors helped too," Bess added.

Just then Nancy noticed Felicity sitting in a corner of the auditorium by herself. She turned to Bess and George. "This is our chance to interview another suspect," she whispered. After Mrs. Corwin and Juliana talked about the

fashion show, Nancy, Bess, and George quietly made their way toward Felicity.

"She's probably angry that the replacement outfits were sewn together so quickly," George said.

When the Clue Crew was just a few feet away from Felicity, she looked up with angry eyes and said, "What do you want?"

"We just wanted to make sure you were all right," Bess said.

"You look really upset about something," Nancy said.

"Do you want to talk about it?" George asked.

Felicity looked at them. "Why would I want to talk about it with you three?" she said.

"Well, for one thing, we're here," Nancy said, "and for another, we don't want you to remember your visit to River Heights as an awful experience."

"Oh, please!" Felicity looked around. "Do you have any idea . . ." She stopped and shook her head. "Of course you don't. You live in this hick town."

"We don't think it's a hick town," George said defensively. "We think it's a great place to live."

"We sure do," Bess added.

"Why are you bothering me?" Felicity said. "Why don't you just leave me alone?"

"Okay, Felicity, we'll be honest with you," Nancy said. "We're not just students, we're also detectives."

"What?" Felicity said. *"Detectives?"*

George nodded. "We've solved a lot of crimes in River Heights," she said.

"In fact, we're trying to solve one now," Bess said.

"Oh, really?" Felicity said. She smirked. "Is somebody's cat missing?"

"That's not funny, Felicity," George said. "We're very serious about crime solving."

"Whatever!" Felicity said.

"We're trying to solve the mystery of the missing clothes," Nancy told her, "and when we do, I think we'll solve the mystery of all the other strange things that have been going on with this fashion show."

"You're talking to the wrong person," Felicity said. "I don't know anything about anything."

"Well, we thought maybe you might have heard or seen something strange," Nancy said.

"Oh, now I get it," Felicity said. "You think I'm guilty."

"We didn't say that," Bess said.

"You didn't have to," Felicity said. She rolled her eyes. "I'm sure you three are nice little girls who—"

"Hey!" George said. "You're the same age we are!"

"In numbers, maybe," Felicity said, "but in sophistication, I'm light-years ahead of all of you."

Oh, brother, Nancy thought. *She is too much.*

"Fine! I'll tell you what I'm angry about," Felicity said. "I told Juliana that I'd do this show because I usually like Juliana's designs, although I think her Rhes! line is really cheap-looking."

Nancy had to bite her tongue to keep from saying anything.

"But right after I signed the contract with Juliana, I had a chance to do a show in Paris, and Juliana wouldn't let me out of my contract," Felicity continued. "I'll probably never again have the chance to go to Paris because I'll forever be associated with this awful-looking Rhes! line."

"Why are they so bad?" Bess asked.

"They're not high fashion, or, as we say in

the business, haute couture," Felicity said, "and that's what models wear on the runways of the world."

"Well, frankly, I think that's a good reason why you might try to ruin the fashion show," George said. "You want to get even with Juliana."

"I'm a professional model," Felicity said. "I'm not a criminal." With that, she turned away, dismissing the Clue Crew.

As Nancy, Bess, and George headed back toward the stage, Nancy said, "Well, I don't like her very much, and I don't agree with what she said about our designs, but I don't think she's our criminal, either."

"Yeah," Bess said. "She was too *honest* about everything."

"I suppose you're right. If she were guilty, she would have been full of excuses and alibis," George said. She sighed. "Now what?"

"Well, we interview our third and last suspect," Bess said.

"We can go to Nadine's house after school," Nancy said.

"We won't have to," George whispered. "Mrs. Nardo just came into the auditorium. She's in the back."

ChaPTER SEVEN

False Alarm

"But why is she here?" George whispered.

"What do you think she's going to do?" Bess whispered back.

"Come on," Nancy said determinedly. "We've got to get this mystery solved before—"

"Nancy! Bess! George!" Juliana shouted. "You're needed onstage!"

"Oh, rats!" Bess said. She looked at Mrs. Nardo. "We may never get another chance to confront her before she tries some other way to destroy the fashion show."

"Of course, we don't really know for sure that she did anything, but you're right, George." Nancy stopped and thought for a minute. "If

51

Nadine's not in the show, why is she here?"

"Girls! Girls!" Mrs. Corwin called. "Juliana needs you! You're on!"

Nancy, Bess, and George ran to the steps that led to the stage. Juliana was already in the wings, giving the professional models some last-minute information, when Nancy, Bess, and George got there.

Nicole smiled at them.

The other models rolled their eyes.

For the next several minutes, when Juliana called out the names of the designer outfits, the models wearing them walked to the center of the stage, turned around in a circle, then started down the runway, which had been built in the center aisle of the auditorium.

When it was Nancy's turn, she felt awkward at first. By the time she got to the middle of the stage, though, she was in sync with the music. Hearing her name as one of the designers of the Mystery Girls! label made her swell with pride. She did her best to remember all the tips Nicole

had given them about how models should walk on the runway.

Nancy thought the other student models did very well too.

Finally the rehearsal was over, and everyone broke for lunch in the cafeteria.

When Nancy, Bess, George, Deirdre, and Quincy entered the cafeteria, everyone applauded, and Nancy had to admit that she really did feel like a celebrity. Some of the second graders even came up and asked for autographs.

They had almost finished eating and were reviewing their spelling words when Nancy saw Mrs. Nardo enter a door at the opposite end of the cafeteria and head toward a far table. Nancy turned and saw Nadine slumped over her tray.

"This isn't looking good," Nancy said to Bess and George. "Mrs. Nardo looks angry, and Nadine looks upset."

"Well, I'd be upset too," Deirdre complained, "if my mother was trying to destroy a fashion show that the whole world was going to watch."

Nancy, Bess, and George looked at her.

"How did you find that out, Deirdre?" Nancy asked.

"Hey! You three are the detectives!" Deirdre said. "You should be telling me."

"Mrs. Nardo is really angry that Nadine isn't in the show," Quincy said. "You should have seen the looks she gave me when I was walking the runway."

"I suspected her all along," Deirdre said.

"Well, why didn't you say something?" Bess said. "We're detectives. We're not mind readers."

Deirdre shrugged. "I'm sorry," she said. "I guess that I just didn't really want to believe it."

"Mrs. Nardo is on our list of suspects," Nancy said. "We're going to question her after school."

When the River Heights models got back to the auditorium, Mrs. Corwin said, "Juliana thinks we're okay for today. So why don't you all go on back to Mrs. Ramirez's classroom?"

"Are you sure?" George asked. "I don't think I have my walk down right."

"You're great, George," Juliana said.

"Well, what about me?" Deirdre said. "I don't want to do anything that will ruin my career."

"Oh, you won't," Juliana said. "In fact, you all did very well."

With Juliana's compliments ringing in their ears, the River Heights models left the auditorium.

The rest of the class was drawing maps of

Africa, but Mrs. Ramirez put Nancy, George, Bess, Deirdre, and Quincy at a table in the back of the room and gave them their spelling quiz. After that they finished out the rest of the day doing their geography assignment.

Before they left school, Nancy used the telephone in the principal's office to call Hannah to tell her that they were going to Nadine Nardo's house to talk to Nadine's mother. Hannah said she would notify Bess's and George's parents.

Just as Nancy, Bess, and George got to the Nardos' house, they heard a scream from the backyard.

"Oh no!" Nancy said. "I wonder what's wrong?"

"This doesn't look good," George whispered.

"We need to find out, and quick!" Bess said.

They rushed through the side gate. Just as they rounded a corner of the house, there was another scream.

In the middle of the yard, standing under a huge tree, were Nadine, Mrs. Nardo, and Nadine's younger sister, Rachel. Suddenly there was another bloodcurdling scream. It had come from Rachel.

"Wow!" Bess said. "That kid has a voice!"

"What's wrong, Nadine?" Nancy called.

"Rachel's parakeet escaped," Nadine said. "My cat has it in her mouth."

Mrs. Nardo looked at Rachel. "Rachel, you're

scaring them both to death," she said. "Nadine promised you that Belle wouldn't eat Ralphie. She's trying to rescue him for you."

That didn't seem to calm Rachel. She let out another scream. It was evidently too much for Belle, though, because she bounded down the tree, walked up to Nadine, and let her take Ralphie out of her mouth.

As everyone headed inside, Nadine whispered, "It's like this every day."

Inside, Mrs. Nardo offered everyone homemade ice cream.

"What brings you girls to our house?" Mrs. Nardo asked. She laughed. "Is there a mystery on our block?"

Nancy looked at Bess and George then back at Mrs. Nardo. "Well, we were hoping that you could help us with that," she said. She had already figured out how to question Mrs. Nardo without her getting suspicious. "We saw you at the rehearsal today. We were wondering if you noticed anything suspicious. We're trying to solve the mystery of who's trying to ruin the fashion show."

Mrs. Nardo laughed. "You're not going to believe this, but I was so angry when Nadine wasn't chosen as one of the models, I thought about doing it myself, but I would never do something awful like that," she said. "I just wanted my beautiful girl to walk the runway."

"Oh, Mama! I told you a thousand times that I wasn't really interested," Nadine said. She looked at Nancy, Bess, and George. "Mama always wanted to be a fashion model herself. Unfortunately, it didn't work out that way."

Mrs. Nardo gave a big sigh. "I guess I was trying to live my dream through Nadine," she said. "I'm sorry if anyone thought I was too pushy."

"We never heard any complaints," George said. She looked at Nancy and Bess. "Did we?"

Nancy and Bess shook their heads.

"Well, we just came over here on the slight chance you might have seen some suspicious activity this morning," Nancy said. "We're following every possible lead."

Just then the telephone rang, and Mrs. Nardo answered it. "Nancy, it's for you," she said. "It's Hannah."

Nancy took the receiver, listened for a few minutes, and then hung up. "Guess what?" she asked. "Mrs. Corwin just called Hannah and said that some of the models' personal belongings have disappeared, and they're blaming River Heights students for the thefts."

CHAPTER EIGHT

Look What I Found!

When Nancy, Bess, and George arrived at school the next morning, there was a crowd of students on the playground. Several were holding up signs that said MODELS, GO HOME! and RHES STUDENTS DON'T STEAL and CANCEL THE FASHION SHOW!

"Oh no!" Nancy said. "This can't be happening!"

When the students saw Nancy, Bess, and George, they immediately rushed toward them.

"Nancy, the Clue Crew has to solve this mystery," one boy said. "Those awful models are accusing us of things we didn't do."

Nancy didn't know what to do. With

Mrs. Nardo, they had exhausted their list of suspects. "We're on it," was all she could say. She was glad the first bell hadn't rung yet. She wanted to find out from the models exactly what had happened.

Nancy pulled Bess and George through the crowd to the front door of the school and went inside.

As they headed toward Mrs. Corwin's classroom, Nicole rushed up to meet them. "Oh, Nancy, I am so sorry," she said breathlessly. "I tried to convince the other models that the River Heights students would never steal their belongings, but they wouldn't listen to me."

"I won't say that we're all perfect here, Nicole," Nancy said, "but RHES students are honest."

"We most certainly are!" Bess and George said in unison.

"Where are the models now?" Nancy asked.

"Juliana's talking to them in the auditorium," Nicole said. "They want to leave. They want to cancel the show. They don't feel safe."

"What?" Nancy, Bess, and George cried.

"I know, I know," Nicole said, rolling her eyes. "They're so used to everyone telling them how wonderful they are all the time that they don't know how to deal with reality."

Nancy shook her head in dismay.

When they got to the auditorium, Nancy saw Juliana whispering something to Mrs. Corwin. The other models were sitting together in a far corner. When they saw Nancy, Bess, George, and Nicole approaching, Felicity said, "Well, well, well, if it isn't River Heights's answer to the FBI." The other models laughed. "Why aren't you out looking for the things your classmates stole from us?"

"What's missing?" Nancy asked.

Cory handed her a list. "I understand that crooks in hick towns like this take their stolen goods to pawnshops," he said nastily. "You might start there first."

"Thanks for the advice," Nancy said. She looked over the list. "We'll be in touch." To Nicole, she whispered, "I think we'll search the school first. I have a feeling that none of these things ever left the building."

"Okay," Nicole whispered back. "I'll try to smooth things over here."

"Thanks, Nicole," Bess said.

Nancy checked with Mrs. Corwin to make sure they wouldn't be needed for the next few minutes. Then the Clue Crew left the auditorium.

Just as they were heading down the third-grade hall, Amanda Johnson came running up to them. "Nancy, you're not going to believe this!" she said. She thrust a large paper sack at her. "Mrs. Ramirez just found these things! They were hidden in some boxes stacked inside the cloakroom! She thinks it's the stuff that was stolen from the models."

Nancy opened the sack. "It is!" she said. She looked at Bess and George. "How are we going to explain this?"

As they headed back toward the auditorium, Bess said, "You don't think someone in our class really did this, do you?"

"I don't know what to think, Bess," Nancy said.

"If we don't solve this soon, though," George said, "no one will ever trust the Clue Crew again."

Nancy nodded.

When they got to the auditorium, the models were practicing their runway walks. When Nicole got to the end of the runway, Nancy whispered, "We found the missing things!"

Nicole blinked, then whispered back, "That's super!"

In a few minutes Nicole joined them. "Where were they?" she asked.

"Hidden inside boxes in Mrs. Ramirez's cloakroom," Bess said.

"That's *our* classroom," George added.

"Oh, that's too bad," Nicole said. "Well, let me have the sack, and I'll return everything to the models."

"Oh, Nicole, thank you so much!" Nancy said.

Juliana suddenly called, "Nancy, Bess, George, Deirdre, and Quincy, come up onstage, please!"

For the rest of the morning, the River Heights models practiced their walks and their outfit changes.

During the lunch break, Nancy said, "Why don't you eat with us, Nicole?"

"Oh, I'd love to," Nicole said. "And please don't worry. The other models were so happy to get their things back that they won't file a police report."

"That's good to know," Nancy said.

Mrs. Corwin had arranged for all the models to get their cafeteria trays and take them to the teacher's lounge so they could eat in peace. The River Heights models and Nicole sat in one corner of the room. The other models sat in a far corner. Juliana and Mrs. Corwin sat in the middle.

"You must lead a really interesting life," Bess said to Nicole. "What's a typical day like?"

Nicole began describing her life as a fashion model. "Of course, there aren't as many fashion shows for tweens and teens as there are for adults," she said, "so I'm hoping all this pays off and that I get picked up by one of the really top modeling agencies. I want to go to Paris and Rome."

"Oh, that is so exciting," Nancy said.

"It would be even more exciting if I could model some of my mother's designs," Nicole said. "Unfortunately, she's not having much luck placing them with a top fashion designer."

"That's too bad," George said.

Later, back in the auditorium, Nancy declared, "After ten walk-throughs and outfit changes, I'm getting really tired." She looked at her watch. "It's almost time for school to be out. I wish we'd stop for today."

"Yeah! I never thought I'd say this, but I'd rather be in class," Bess agreed. "This is really hard work."

"I thought I was in better shape than this," George said. "I may need to play more soccer."

Juliana shouted, "Okay! Okay! We'll stop for a couple hours, but I want everyone back here at seven p.m. The show is tomorrow, and we still have a few things we need to work on."

"Look what I found!" Everyone turned. Nicole was standing at the back of the auditorium. She had a pile of clothes in her hands. "It's all the missing outfits!"

"Oh, wonderful, Nicole!" Juliana said. "We really don't need them now for the River Heights show, but I do want to use them for the New York show!"

The Clue Crew rushed over to Nicole.

"Where did you find them?" Nancy asked.

"In one of the gymnasium lockers," Nicole

said. "I was just wandering around, trying to clear my head, and all of a sudden I saw a piece of blue cloth sticking out from the bottom of a door, so I opened it, and there they were!"

"Bring them here, Nicole!" Juliana called. "I want to see if they're all right."

When Nicole was out of earshot, Nancy turned to Bess and George and said, "That's strange. We searched those lockers ourselves, and we didn't find anything."

ChAPTER NiNE

The Last Rehearsal

As the models began their last rehearsal for the fashion show, Nancy simply could not shake the feeling that the one final clue that would solve the mystery was right under their noses.

Nancy struggled to concentrate on all the last-minute details about successful modeling that Nicole kept telling them. Unfortunately her brain simply would not let her think about anything else except the case.

Suddenly Nancy stumbled and almost fell off the runway.

"Nancy!" Nicole cried.

Bess and George rushed to Nancy's side.

"Are you all right?" Bess said. "Is anything broken?"

Nancy struggled to sit up. "I'm fine. I'm fine! Nothing's broken!" She looked around. Everyone was staring at her. "How embarrassing," she whispered to George.

Just then Nicole reached them.

"I'm sorry, Nicole," Nancy said. "I'm not normally this clumsy. It's just that—"

"Oh, Nancy, please don't worry. You're doing fine," Nicole interrupted her. "I'm just glad you didn't break your leg!"

"Me too," Nancy said. George and Bess helped her up.

"Let's just restart your runway walk," Nicole said.

"Thank you," Nancy said.

As the girls headed back behind the curtain, they heard Nicole shout, "Cue up the music for the River Heights models from the beginning, all right?"

"She is so nice," Bess said when they reached the wings. "I'm glad she's the one helping us and not the other models."

"She really is nice! The other models would probably have pushed Nancy the rest of the way off the runway," George said. "We're lucky she's on our side."

Nancy couldn't believe it. That was exactly what had been puzzling her. Nicole was nice, all right! In fact, she seemed *too* nice!

"I wonder why," Nancy said.

George and Bess looked at her.

"Why *what*?" Bess asked.

"Why is Nicole so nice to us?" Nancy said. "Is it just a cover to hide what she's really doing?"

Bess and George blinked in unison.

"Are you thinking what I think you're think-ing?" George said.

"Well, we've exhausted all the other suspects," Nancy said. "After all, she found the missing clothes in a place where we had already looked. Maybe her being nice is to keep us from suspect-ing that—"

"Nancy Drew!" Bess said. "Nicole isn't a criminal, she's a model!"

Nancy sighed. "I hope you're right," she said.

The day of the big River Heights fashion show finally arrived. Nancy, Bess, George, and Deirdre met in a room separate from the other models. Quincy had a curtained-off area next to them, and Peter had agreed to help him make fast changes.

Nancy looked at her watch. "It's almost time," she said. "I have butterflies!"

"So do we!" the others said.

Suddenly there was a knock on the door.

When Deirdre opened it, Nicole was standing there.

"You look gorgeous!" Bess said.

Nicole smiled. "Well, I forgot to tell you something," she said. "You will need a special kind of makeup for the television lights. Otherwise, your faces fade out, and no one can tell who you are."

"Oh, that can't happen!" Deirdre said. "I want people to recognize me. It's important for my career!"

"Where can we get it?" Nancy asked.

"Follow me," Nicole said.

They followed Nicole down a hallway to a small room. "I've set up the makeup in here," she said. "Put it on and then stand outside this door until you're called."

"Thanks, Nicole," Deirdre said. "You're super!"

Nicole smiled again. "I'll see you later," she said.

Everyone quickly started applying the special makeup. Peter helped a reluctant Quincy with his.

Just as they finished, a harried stage director burst inside. "I've been looking all over for you!" he shouted. "Line up! You're on now!"

As they ran down the hallway after the stage director Nancy tried to explain about the makeup.

"Stop talking!" the stage director said. "You're late! Let's move!"

As they lined up they passed Felicity and

Cory, who looked at them and started laughing.

"What's their problem?" Bess asked from the middle of the line.

"They're just jealous," Deirdre said.

All of a sudden Nancy had a peculiar feeling. She hoped Deirdre was right.

CHAPTER TEN

Who Would Have Guessed?

This is it, Nancy thought as she quickly stepped through the narrow curtain opening and onto the runway. Bess, George, and Quincy were right behind her. Deirdre wanted to be last so she would get the most applause.

Just as the bright lights hit her, Nancy smiled, thinking there would be thunderous applause. Instead, there was loud laughter, and Nancy wondered what in the world was wrong.

Maybe it's just happy laughter,

Nancy thought as she continued to smile and walk the way Nicole had taught them.

When Nancy was almost to the end of the runway, though, she was sure they weren't laughing with her.

At the end of the runway, out of most of the bright lights, Nancy could now see into the audience. People weren't just laughing, they were pointing, too!

You don't understand fashion, Nancy thought. She held her head high. She was glad she was part of this international fashion show.

Nancy made her turn to head back to the stage, and right away she knew what was making everyone laugh. Bess, George, Quincy, and Deirdre all had bright orange faces! They looked like pumpkin heads. Nancy was sure she looked like one too!

How did this happen? Nancy wondered.

Then all of a sudden the pieces of the puzzle fit.

Finally Nancy reached the opening in the curtain, went through it, and, when she was totally out of sight of the audience, exhaled.

What a mean, terrible thing to do! Nancy thought.

As the rest of the show continued, Bess, George, Quincy, and Deirdre rushed over to her.

"Why are our faces orange?" Deirdre demanded. "My career is ruined!"

"You were right, Nancy," George said.

"I still can't believe it," Bess added.

"What are you two talking about?" Quincy asked.

Just then Nicole came over to them. "Oh, I'm so sorry! I don't know what happened. There must have been some mix-up—or maybe the makeup is just old!"

Nancy and the Crew Clue just looked at her for a few moments, and then Nancy said, "Really? I don't think that's it at all, Nicole. I think you did it on purpose. The only question is *Why.*"

"What do you mean?" Nicole said. "Are you accusing me of all the pranks?"

"That's exactly what we're doing, Nicole," Bess said.

"We had already searched those lockers where you found the missing clothes," George said. "That couldn't have been where they were hidden."

"That gave you away," Nancy added, "but I guess we just didn't want to believe it."

"Well, I . . . I . . . ," Nicole started to say, and then she burst into tears. "It's not my fault. My mother is a wonderful designer, and Juliana won't . . ."

"Girls! Girls! It's incredible!"

Everyone turned. Juliana was hurrying toward them. With her was Mrs. Corwin, Mrs. Ramirez, and a woman Nancy didn't recognize.

"We're sorry, Juliana," Nancy said. "We were just talking about . . ."

"Sorry? Sorry for *what*?" Juliana said. "This was the grandest fashion show I've ever put on! Several buyers from stores around the world are going to carry my Rhes! line of clothing."

Nancy and the others looked at one another.

"Really?" Nancy said.

"But what about the orange makeup?" Deirdre asked.

"That was a fantastic idea," the woman said.

"Oh, I'm sorry, students. This is Sophia Napoli," Juliana said. "She's the editor of *Fashion Plate* magazine, and she's going to do a story about my Rhes! designs."

"I thought the orange makeup really went

well with every outfit," Sophia said. "In fact, that's going to be the focus of the article: 'Why can't we wear different colors of makeup if we feel like it?'"

"That's what I'm saying!" Deirdre said.

Everyone laughed—including Nicole.

That night everyone connected with the fashion show met at Nancy's favorite pizza parlor for dinner. They took up several tables.

In the middle of the meal, Nicole stood up and said, "I want to apologize to everyone for the things I did. I hid the designs, I hid the clothing, I hid the personal belongings of the other models, and I substituted the orange makeup for the regular makeup. It's just a light shade of orange until the runway lights hit it, and then it turns really bright!" She looked at Juliana. "I'm sorry. I was angry that you didn't use my mother's designs—because she's a wonderful designer."

"Oh, Nicole!" Juliana said. "I *am* going to use

your mother's designs!" She shook her head. "It's just that I've been so busy getting ready for the River Heights show, I hadn't said anything about it."

"Juliana! Mother will be so happy!" Nicole said. "I'm so sorry. That was *very* unprofessional of me!" She smiled. "But I think the River Heights models were as professional as any models I've ever seen." She turned to Felicity, Elizabeth, Marissa, and Cory. "Don't you agree?"

This time, they all nodded and smiled.

"Oh, I just knew this was my career!" Deirdre said.

"Well, I never thought about a career in modeling," Nancy said, "but it really was fun!"

"I have an idea," Nicole said. "Anytime you want to come to New York, you can stay with me and my mother, and we'll take you to some of the famous fashion houses."

Deirdre gasped. "Do you think when they see me they'll want me to model for them?"

"You never can tell," Nicole said.

"Here's to a successful fashion show—and a successfully solved case," toasted Juliana.

Everyone cheered.

D-I-Y Design

You're going to become a famous fashion designer and hit the catwalk!

You will need:
Paper

Colored pencils

Magazines and catalogs for inspiration

Let's get started!

❀ Sketch a body template onto a blank sheet of paper. Make as many photocopies of this template as you want so you don't have to redraw it when you make a new design.

❀ With the colored pencils, create a variety of outfits. You can draw them all for one season (like fall) or for one activity (like ballet).

❀ When you've finished, print or sign your name

on the design so that people will know you are the designer.

❀ Finally, tape up the designs around your room, and invite family or friends to see your latest collection!

Be creative. Draw the kinds of clothes you want to wear yourself!

NaNcy DReW aND The CLUE CReW

Test your detective skills with more Clue Crew cases!

FROM ALaDDiN • PUBLiSheD By SiMON & SChUSTeR